The Love Story of
Eros and Psyche

Mythology gives you interesting explanations about life and satisfies your curiosity with stories that have been made up to explain surprising or frightening phenomena. People throughout the world have their own myths. In the imaginary world of mythology, humans can become birds or stars. The sun, wind, trees, and the rest of the natural world are full of gods who often interact with humans.

Greek and Roman mythology began more than 3,000 years ago. It consisted of stories first told by Greeks that lived on the shores of the Mediterranean Sea. In Italy the Romans would later borrow and modify many of these stories.

Most of the Greek myths were related to gods that resided upon the cloud-shrouded Mount Olympus. These clouds frequently could create a mysterious atmosphere on Mount Olympus. The ancient Greeks thought that their gods dwelt there and had human shapes, feelings, and behavior.

The Greeks and the Romans built temples, offered animal sacrifices, said prayers, performed plays, and competed in sports to please their humanlike gods on Mount Olympus.

How did the world come into being in the first place?

Why is there night and day?

How did the four seasons come into existence?

Where do we go after we die?

Reading Greek and Roman mythology can help you understand ancient human ideas about our world. Since many Western ideas originated with the Greeks and Romans, you will benefit from taking a look into the mythology that helped to shape those important classical cultures. Understanding their mythology will give you an interesting view of the world you live in.

Aphrodite ▶ ▶ ▶

She was the goddess of beauty. Out of jealous spite for Psyche's beauty, Aphrodite ordered her son Eros to punish Psyche.

Eros

He was the god of love and son of Aphrodite, the goddess of beauty. Smitten by Psyche's beauty, Eros fell in love with her.

Zephyr ▶ ▶ ▶

He was the god of the wind and carried the two sisters of Psyche to the Castle of Eros.

Demeter ▶ ▶ ▶

She was the goddess of agriculture and fertility. Feeling sorry for Psyche, Demeter told her the best way to find Eros.

Psyche

She was a mortal princess who was more beautiful than the goddesses. Aphrodite hated Psyche's great beauty. Psyche fell in love with Eros, who was ordered by Aphrodite to punish her for being so beautiful.

Persephone

She was the daughter of Zeus and Demeter. Originally, Persephone was the goddess of the harvest with her mother; however, she became the goddess of the Underworld after she was abducted by Hades, the god of the Underworld.

Zeus

He was the king of the gods and had supreme authority on Mount Olympus and on earth. Zeus used thunderbolts as weapons because they were capable of destroying anything.

Pleasure

She was the daughter of Eros and Psyche.

Psyche, a mortal maiden, was more beautiful than Aphrodite, the goddess of beauty. She aroused the anger of Aphrodite. Aphrodite could not stand losing her reputation to a mere mortal, so she ordered her son Eros to punish Psyche. Her intention was to make beautiful Psyche fall in love with a monster, making her a fool in front of people. However, stunned by Psyche s beauty, Eros fell in love with her.

A mysterious love story of a god and a human— the love story of Eros and Psyche—begins this way.

However, as much as it is beautiful, the love story of a god and a mortal entails ordeals and sufferings.

Deeply in love with Psyche, Eros married her, but he had to conceal his true appearance. Moved by the gentleness and warmth of Eros, Psyche also fell in love with him.

However, sadly, she had to promise that she could not and must not see the face of her beloved husband, Eros. Finally, poor Psyche fell for the tricks of her sisters. In order to have a better look at sleeping Eros, she accidentally allowed a drop of hot oil to fall upon him. Psyche's human foolishness inflicted suffering on herself.

Then, how does the love story of Eros and Psyche develop? Will Eros forgive foolish Psyche, and will they live happily every after? Or will something new and terrible happen?

Contents

1

The Princess Psyche

The youngest daughter, Psyche,
was the prettiest.

Once, there was a king who had three beautiful daughters.

Many handsome young men traveled from far away to marry these beautiful women. The youngest daughter, Psyche, was the

prettiest.
People from
many
countries
would walk for
weeks just to
look at her.

Aphrodite, the goddess of beauty,

became jealous.

Men were ignoring her.

They only wanted to look at Psyche.

Soon Aphrodite's temples were empty.

Aphrodite decided to punish Psyche.

Aphrodite told her son, Eros,

"You must punish Psyche.

She made people forget about me.

I am the goddess of beauty!

Make Psyche fall in love with an ugly,

disgusting creature.

Then everyone will laugh at her."

Eros went to Aphrodite's garden.
He found two fountains there.
One had sweet water and
the other had bitter water.
The sweet water made women
more beautiful.
The bitter water was dangerous.
If a woman touched the bitter water,
no man would ever love her.
Eros had two bottles.
He put sweet water in one and bitter water
in the other.

Eros went to Psyche's bedroom.

She was sleeping.

As soon as he saw her, Eros was filled with
love for the beautiful woman.

He felt sorry to make trouble for her,
but Eros had to obey Aphrodite.

So he put a few drops of bitter water
on her lips.

He then pushed her arm with his arrow.

Suddenly, Psyche woke up,
but she could not see Eros
because he was invisible.

Eros was very surprised when he saw
Psyche's beautiful eyes.

When Psyche sat up, Eros jumped away
from her bed.
He fell down and hurt himself
on his own arrow.
He jumped up and poured the sweet water
over Psyche's hair.
The mixture of the sweet and bitter water
was terrible for Psyche.
She became more beautiful,
but now no man would ever love her.

Over the months that followed, the young
princess became very sad and lonely.
She waited for a handsome young man to
come and ask her to marry him,
but no one ever did.

Her two elder sisters married two young
princes who were brothers.
They moved into the princes' castle.
Now Psyche was alone.
Psyche became lonelier and lonelier.

Psyche's
parents
believed
the gods were
angry at Psyche.
A woman
should never
be as
beautiful as a goddess.

They went to Apollo's temple for advice.
"Your daughter will never marry any man,"
the oracle said.
"Instead, she will go to the top of a
mountain.
There she will become the wife of a terrible
monster."

Psyche's parents began to cry.
They promised Psyche that they would
never allow her to marry a monster.
But Psyche thought that she could not
escape her fate.
She prepared to go to a nearby mountain.
She had heard that a monster lived
there near the peak.

2

The Love of
Eros and Psyche

One happy evening, they got married
in their dark bedroom.

Psyche climbed the mountain.
She felt like the loneliest girl in the
world.

Suddenly, she was
blown into the air by
Zephyr, the god of
the west wind.
Zephyr gently
carried Psyche
to a nearby
meadow
surrounded
by mountains.

The young princess blinked her eyes
and looked around.
She did not see the cave of some terrible
monster.
To her right, she saw a fountain
surrounded by trees.
To her left, she saw a huge palace
on a hillside.

When she walked inside the palace, she
noticed furniture, sculptures and paintings.
Everything was beautifully made.

05

From somewhere in the castle,
she heard voices.
The voices were talking to her,
but she couldn't see anyone.
The voices said, "All that you see is yours.
We are your servants.
We will do anything you ask.
Why don't you lie down in your room
and rest?
When you are ready, take a bath
and then
come to the
dining
room."

Psyche did as the voice suggested.

When she came to the dining room,

she saw a chair flying through the air.

It was placed in front of the table for her.

Invisible hands brought her delicious food

and delightful wines.

An invisible orchestra began to play

soothing music.

Invisible Servants Serving Psyche

 06 After eating,

Psyche returned to her bedroom.

She sat down in the dark.

Soon she heard a soft voice.

This one was different from the others.

This voice was gentle and loving.

The voice said that he was the owner

of the castle.

"Please, do not be
afraid of me.
I'm not a monster.
I'm a god.
I'll only visit you
at night when it's
dark, because a
person can't look at a
god.
I've brought you here because I love you.
I've loved you from the first time I saw you.
I want to marry you.
Sadly, you'll never be able to see me.
However, I will be with you here in this
room every night."
It was actually Eros,
but he did not tell Psyche his name.
Psyche felt a peace.
She quickly fell into a deep sleep.

When Psyche woke up the next morning,
she realized that she was alone.
When she came out of her bedroom,
the voices told Psyche to relax in her new
home.
She was served by the invisible servants
all day.

Day after day, the servants helped Psyche.
Every night the god spoke to her in the
bedroom.

He always spoke kind and loving words
to her.
After some time, Psyche grew to love Eros.

She loved him even though she could not
see him.
She thought his voice was enough.
They were happy and comfortable together.

One happy evening, they got married
in their dark bedroom.

In the palace, Psyche needed nothing.
Everything that she wanted was given
to her.
But soon Psyche became bored.
She wanted to visit her parents and her
sisters.

One night, Psyche said to her husband,
Eros, "I love you and I want to stay with
you forever in this beautiful palace.
But my life here is boring during the day.
I want to see my parents and my sisters.
I want to tell them that I am happy and
healthy.
I want to tell them about you,
my kind husband.
Most of all, I don't want them to worry
about me."

Eros
understood Psyche.
He agreed to
bring Psyche's two sisters
to his castle.
He ordered Zephyr to fly to
the sisters and bring them back.

When Psyche met her sisters,
she hugged them and cried.
"Please," Psyche said.
"Come with me into my home.
Everything you need is here.
Tonight we'll have a feast to
celebrate our reunion."
Psyche showed her
sisters around
the beautiful
palace.
They saw the
finely
decorated
rooms, the
sculptures,
and the
treasure
chests.

They became jealous.

During dinner Psyche's sisters asked

Psyche about her husband.

They thought it was strange that he had

not introduced himself to them yet.

"He's a handsome young prince,"
said Psyche.
"You may not see him during your stay
here. He usually hunts all day long.
He comes back to the palace late at night,"
Psyche said.
The sisters, however, were not satisfied.
"We must see your husband
and talk to him.
We must tell mother and father
about your husband."
Psyche could not lie to her parents
and her sisters.
"Frankly speaking, I've never seen my
husband," she said.
"He only enters my room late at night
when it's dark.
And he leaves before dawn.
No matter how much I ask,
he won't allow me to see his face."

"It must be true then," said one of Psyche's sisters. "He must be a terrible monster. Why doesn't he allow you to see his face?
Some people told me that a monster lives nearby.
Maybe your husband is this monster!
We must find out!"

"Hide a lantern and a sharp knife in your bedroom. Wait for your husband to fall asleep. Then shine the light upon his face. If he is really a horrible monster, you must kill him. Then you will be free to return to us."

Psyche didn't believe that her husband was a monster. But she did think it was strange that he wouldn't allow her to see him. So she decided to hide a lantern in the bedroom.

That night, when her husband
was asleep, she lit the lantern
and held it up.
She didn't see a terrible monster.
She saw a very handsome young god.
He had golden hair,
white skin and two large
snow-white wings.

Psyche realized that her husband was
Eros.
She was charmed by his handsome face.
Her heart began to beat rapidly.
She bent down for a closer look.
Then a drop of hot oil from
Psyche's lantern fell onto Eros's chest.

Psyche Holds a Lantern

3

Psyche's Punishments

"You will have to work hard
before I forgive you."

Eros woke up. Without
saying a word, he stood up and
flew out of the window.
"Oh, foolish Psyche! Why
did you need to see me?
It seems that you
trust your silly sisters
more than your husband.
Go, and spend the rest of your life with
them.
A marriage can't last without trust,"
he said.
Eros then flew away,
leaving Psyche lying on the floor, crying.

Instantly Psyche found herself
in an open field.
Her sisters' castle was nearby.
She went inside and told them the whole
story.

The sisters pretended to be sad for Psyche,
but they were actually very happy.
They thought perhaps Eros would now
choose one of them to marry him.

The next morning,
the two sisters woke up
and packed
their bags quietly.
They both planned
to go to Eros's castle.
The first sister left early.
When she reached
the top of the hill,
she called for Zephyr.
She jumped off the hill.
She thought Zephyr
would catch her and
take her to Eros.
But Zephyr was not there.
She fell a long way and died.

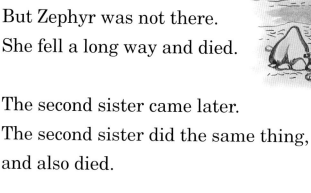

The second sister came later.
The second sister did the same thing,
and also died.

12

After some time,
Psyche recovered from her sadness.
She decided to find her husband and ask
for forgiveness.
She promised herself that she wouldn't
rest until she found Eros.

Early one morning,
Psyche packed her bags and left.
A few weeks later, she came to a high
mountain with
a temple
at the top.
Psyche
thought that
perhaps
her husband
lived there.
So, she entered
the holy place.

Inside, she saw corn and barley all over
the floor.

There were also farmer's tools lying around
in a mess.

Psyche felt so bad that such a beautiful
temple was messy.

Since she was a religious woman.

She began to sweep up the corn and barley
and pick up the farmer's tools.

The temple belonged to the goddess
Demeter.
At that moment, she was passing by.
She felt great pity for Psyche who was
working hard to clean her temple.
"Psyche, I see that you have suffered lately.
I want to help you.
However, I can't
stop Aphrodite
from being angry
with you."
"The best thing that
I can do is to give
you this advice.
Go to her temple.
Tell her that you
respect her
and ask for forgiveness.
Perhaps, she will allow you to see her son,
Eros again."

Psyche went to the temple of Aphrodite.
The goddess seemed very angry with her.
"Have you come to worship me?"
asked Aphrodite.
"Or maybe you want to see your husband
instead of me.

My poor boy has a broken
heart because of you.
I will punish you.
You will have to
work hard
before I forgive you.
Then perhaps
you can see
your husband
again."

Aphrodite showed Psyche a great heap of
beans, wheat, barley and other grains.
"You must separate these grains.
Put each kind of grain in separate bags.
You must finish before nightfall."
Aphrodite left.

Psyche fell to the ground, crying.
She knew that she could not do this job.

A little ant felt sorry for Psyche.

He asked the other ants to help the

beautiful woman.

The other ants agreed.

The queen ant organized her workers

into teams.

Each team was supposed to gather

a certain kind of grain.

The ants marched to the grains

like an army.

They carried the grains into their

proper bags.

At dusk, the job was finished.

Aphrodite returned from her supper.

She was disappointed to see that Psyche
had done the job.

"You clearly didn't do this by yourself.

My son must have helped you somehow!"

Aphrodite threw a piece of rotten bread to
Psyche and walked away.

The next morning, Aphrodite brought
Psyche to a nearby riverbank.
"You'll find rams with golden fleeces
on the other side of this river.
Take a little wool from every one of those
animals.
Make sure you bring it back to me
before nightfall."

Psyche walked back
and forth trying
to find some way
to cross the fast
and deep waters.
Suddenly, the river
god spoke to her.
"Don't try to cross
the river now, dear Psyche.

If you do make it across, the rams will try
to hurt you.
They like to hurt people with their teeth
and their horns.
Wait until noon when the river calms.
At that time of day, you'll be able to cross
easily.
On the other side, you'll find the rams fast
asleep.
On the bushes and the tree trunks,
you'll find plenty of golden wool."

Psyche followed this advice.

Soon she had gathered a lot of golden wool.

She brought it back to Aphrodite.

The goddess was not pleased that Psyche finished this job.

"Once again, I guess that somebody helped you."

"I want you to do one more thing for me.
Go to the underworld and find the goddess
Persephone.
Tell her that I have sent you to collect some
of her beauty.
I have lost some of my own while nursing
my sick son, Eros.
Hurry back.
I must paint my face with her beauty
before the dinner of the gods tonight."

Psyche had to reach
the underworld
immediately.
She knew only one
way to get there
quickly.
She would have to
kill herself.
She climbed a high
tower.
Just before she jumped,
she heard a voice.
It said, "Why are you
going to the
underworld
in such a
dangerous
way?"

"I know an easy way to get there on foot."
The voice also told her how to convince the ferryman to take her across the river Styx.
The voice told Psyche of a path in a cave. This path went past the three-headed dog that guards the entrance to the underworld.

"But be careful," the voice said, "Persephone will give you a box containing her beauty. You must not look into it. No matter how curious you are, don't look into the box."

Psyche did exactly as the voice told her.
When she reached the underworld,
Persephone greeted her warmly.
The goddess was happy to help her.
She gave Psyche a box.
Psyche thanked Persephone politely.

Then, she turned to walk up the path that
she had just come down.
She walked safely back to the world.

On the long walk back,

Psyche became curious about the box.

Psyche stared at it for a long time.

Finally she thought,

'I got the box so I should be able to use

some of the beauty.

If I make myself more beautiful,

Eros will love me again.'

Psyche opened the box.

But she didn't find beauty.

Instead, purple gas came out.

It surrounded her head.

It made Psyche fall asleep.

4

Eros's Forgiveness

"I must find my wife."

Meanwhile, Eros had recovered from his broken heart.

He decided that he must forgive Psyche. "I must find my wife," he said.

Eros found Psyche asleep in the middle of the road.

He blew the purple gas away from her head and back into the box.

Eros woke Psyche up.

"You are too curious.

Take this box back to my mother.

I shall ask Zeus to help us get back together."

Eros flew to Zeus.

"Oh! Zeus, king of all gods!

I ask you to make Psyche my wife again.

I know that gods and women should not marry.

but this princess has the manners and the grace and beauty of a goddess,

She would be a good wife for me.

I know that she has many human weaknesses," he continued.

"Psyche's greatest weakness is her curiosity.

This made her look at my face.

But remember, she is curious only because you made women that way."

Eros talked to Zeus for many hours.

Finally, Zeus agreed with Eros.

He called Psyche to the dinner of the gods.

When Psyche arrived,

Zeus gave her a magical cup of wine.

"Drink this, Psyche,

and you shall become a god," he said.

"You and Eros will be husband and wife
again. Both of you will be together until
the end of time."

Taking the cup, Psyche drank all the wine.

58

While angels sang, Eros and Psyche were finally together again.

They are still together even now.

Perhaps the only god who is happier than they are is their daughter.

Her name is 'Pleasure'.

Reading Comprehension

◉ Read and answer the questions.

1. Why were Aphrodite's temples empty?

   (A) Because Aphrodite was jealous.
   (B) Because people preferred to look at Psyche.
   (C) Because Aphrodite was not beautiful.

2. How did Psyche's husband react when she said
   that she wanted to see her family?

   (A) He was sad.
   (B) He was angry.
   (C) He was understanding.

3. What did Psyche see when she lit the lantern
   and held it to Eros's face?

   (A) an ugly monster
   (B) a snowy-white god
   (C) a good-looking god with blond hair

4. How did Psyche's sisters real feeling after listening to the story of her separation from Eros?

(A) They felt sad.
(B) They felt happy.
(C) They were surprised.

5. What did Psyche do in Demeter's temple?

(A) She cleaned the floor.
(B) She worshipped Demeter.
(C) She made a mess.

6. What did Aphrodite tell Psyche to do with the heap of grains?

(A) Make the ants separate them.
(B) Separate the heaps into smaller piles.
(C) Separate the grains and put them into bags.

7. Who carried Psyche to a huge palace on a hillside?

_____

8. What was Psyche's second punishment?

_____

9. What was inside the box that Persephone gave to Psyche?

_____

10. What's the name of Eros and Psyche's daughter?

_____

Read and talk about it.

> . . . They saw the finely decorated rooms, the
> sculptures and the treasure chests. They became
> jealous. . . . The sisters pretended to be sad for Psyche.
> But they were actually very happy. They thought
> perhaps Eros would now choose one of
> them to marry him. . . .

11. Psyche's two sisters hated Psyche because of
    jealousy. Have you ever been jealous?
    If you have, talk about it.

> . . . On the long walk back, Psyche became curious
> about the box. Psyche stared at it for a long time.
> Finally she thought, I got the box so I should be
> able to use some of the beauty.
> If I make myself more beautiful, Eros will love me again.
> Psyche opened the box. . . .

12. Psyche opened the forbidden box, because she
    wanted to be more beautiful.
    What would you have done if you were Psyche?

The Signs of the Zodiac

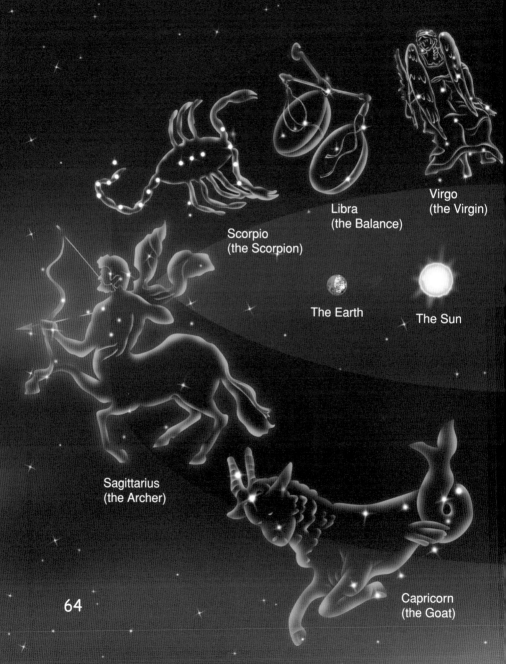

Virgo
(the Virgin)

Libra
(the Balance)

Scorpio
(the Scorpion)

The Earth

The Sun

Sagittarius
(the Archer)

Capricorn
(the Goat)

The word "zodiac" comes from a Greek word meaning, "the circle of animals".
Where did the zodiac come from?
In this section, you can find the Greek Myths that explain the origins of these signs.

Leo
(the Lion)

Cancer
(the Crab)

Gemini
(the Twins)

Taurus
(the Bull)

Aries
(the Ram)

Pisces
(the Fishes)

Aquarius
(the Water Bearer)

Aries (the Ram)

March 21st ~ April 20th

The origin of Aries stems from the Tale of the Golden Ram. The ram safely carried off Phrixus.

Phrixus sacrificed the Golden Ram to Zeus and in turn, Zeus placed the ram in the heavens.

Taurus (the Bull)

April 21st ~ May 20th

The origin of Taurus stems from the Tale of Europa and the Bull. Zeus turned himself into a bull in order to attract Europa to him.

The bull carried Europa across the sea to Crete.

In remembrance, Zeus placed the image of the bull in the stars.

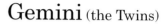

Gemini (the Twins)

May 21st ~ June 21st

This sign stems from the Tale of Castor and Pollux. Castor and Pollux were twins. They both loved each other very much. In honor of the brothers's great love, Zeus placed them among the stars.

Cancer (the Crab)

June 22nd ~ July 22nd

The sign of Cancer stems from one of the 12 Labors of Hercules.

Hera sent the crab to kill Hercules. But Hercules crushed the crab under his foot just before he defeated the Hydra. To honor the crab, Hera placed it among the stars.

Leo (the Lion)

July 23rd ~ August 22nd

The sign of Leo stems from another of Hercules 12 Labors. Hercules's the first labor was to kill a lion that lived in Nemea valley. He killed the Nemea lion with his hands. In remembrance of the grand battle, Zeus placed the Lion of Nemea among the stars.

Virgo (the Virgin)

August 23rd ~ September 22nd

Virgo's origin stems from the Tale of Pandora. Virgo represents the goddess of purity and innocence, Astraea. After Pandora opened the

forbidden box and let loose all the evils into the world, every god went back to heaven. As a remembrance of innocence lost, Astraea was placed amongst the stars in the form of Virgo.

Libra (the Balance)

September 23rd ~ October 21st

The Libra are the scales that balance justice. They are held by the goddess of divine justice, Themis. Libra shines right beside Virgo which represents Astraea, daughter of Themis.

Scorpio (the Scorpion)

October 22nd ~ November 21st

The sign of Scorpio stems from the Tale of Orion. Orion and Artemis were great hunting partners, which made Artemis's brother Apollo very jealous. Apollo pleaded with Gaea to kill Orion. So Gaea created the scorpion and killed great Orion. In remembrance of this act, Zeus placed Orion and the scorpion amongst the stars. But they never appear at the same time.

Sagittarius (the Archer)
November 23rd ~ December 21st

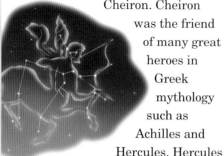

This sign is representative of Cheiron. Cheiron was the friend of many great heroes in Greek mythology such as Achilles and Hercules. Hercules accidentally shot Cheiron in the leg with a poison arrow. Cheiron was immortal so he couldn't die. Instead, he had to endure the unending pain. Cheiron begged Zeus to kill him. To honor Cheiron, Zeus placed him among the stars.

 23

Capricorn (the Goat)
December 22nd ~ January 19th

The sign of Capricorn represents the goat Amalthea who fed the infant Zeus. It's said that Zeus placed her among the stars in gratitude.

Aquarius (the Water Bearer)
January 20th ~ February 18th

The sign of Aquarius stems from the Tale of the Deucalion's Flood. In this tale, Zeus pours all the waters of the heavens onto earth to wash away all the evil creatures. Deucalion and his wife Pyrrha were the only survivors of the great flood.

Pisces (the Fishes)
February 19th ~ March 20th

The Pisces represents the goddess of love & beauty, Aphrodite and her son the god of love, Eros. They were taking a stroll down the Euphrates River when there was a Typhon. They pleaded for Zeus to help them escape, so Zeus changed them into fish and they swam away safely. In remembrance of this, Aphrodite is the big fish constellation and Eros is the small fish constellation.

希臘羅馬神話故事 **7**

愛神和賽姬 Eros and Psyche

First Published April, 2011
First Printing April, 2011

Original Story by Thomas Bulfinch
Rewritten by David O'Flaherty
Illustrated by Gutdva Irina Mixailovna
Designer by Hyeonyoung Kim, Eonju No
Translated by Jia-chen Chuo

Printed and distributed by Cosmos Culture Ltd.
http://www.icosmos.com.tw
Tel: 02-2365-9739
Fax: 02-2365-9835
http://www.icosmos.com.tw
Publisher: Value-Deliver Culture Ltd.

神話以趣味的方式，爲我們生活中的煩惱提出解釋，並滿足我們的好奇心。許多故事的編寫，都是爲了解釋一些令人驚奇或恐懼的現象，因此，世界各地不同的國家、民族，都有屬於自己的神話。

希臘與羅馬神話充滿想像力，並結合了諸神與英雄們激盪人心的傳奇故事，因此特別爲人所津津樂道。希臘與羅馬神話反應了眞實的人類世界，因此，閱讀神話對於瞭解西方文化與思維，有極大的幫助。

這些經典故事的背景，可追溯至史前時代，但對於當代的讀者而言，它們深具魅力的法寶何在？其秘密就在於，神話能超越時空，完整地呈現人類心中的慾望。這些激盪人心的冒險故事，將帶您經歷生命中的各種重要事件：戰爭與和平、生命與死亡、善與惡，以及各種愛恨情仇。

希臘與羅馬神話裡所描繪的諸神，並不全是完美、萬能的天神，他們和人類一樣，會因憤怒而打鬥，會耍詭計戲弄其他天神，會因愛與嫉妒而感到痛苦。在 Let's Enjoy Mythology 系列的第二部 Reading Greek and Roman Mythology in English 中，你將會讀到許多具有人類特質的英雄、女英雄、眾神和女神的故事。

Reading Greek and Roman Mythology in English 將引領你穿越時空，一探想像中的古希臘世界。

前言

　　賽姬是一位凡間的少女，其美麗更勝美神阿芙柔黛蒂，因此觸怒了阿芙柔黛蒂。阿芙柔黛蒂不甘心被一位凡人給比了下去，便派遣其子愛羅斯去懲罰賽姬。她計畫讓賽姬愛上一個怪物，成爲眾人的笑柄。然而，愛羅斯卻被賽姬的美貌所吸引，而愛上了她。

　　一段不可思議的人神之戀——愛羅斯與賽姬的愛情故事——就這樣展開了。

　　但是，人神之戀雖美，卻必須承擔嚴峻的考驗與磨難。

　　深愛著賽姬的愛羅斯娶了她爲妻，卻必須隱藏自己的眞實面貌。賽姬被愛羅斯的溫柔與熱情所打動，也愛上了他。但不幸的是，她必須答應不能看到親愛丈夫的模樣。後來，可憐的賽姬被姊姊們的計謀所騙，想要趁愛羅斯熟睡之時，窺探他的模樣，卻不小心將油燈的熱油滴在他身上。她的凡人之愚，爲她自己帶來了痛苦。

　　接下來，愛羅斯與賽姬的愛情故事又是如何發展的呢？愛羅斯能原諒愚蠢的賽姬，兩人能就此過著幸福快樂的日子嗎？還是有什麼全新、可怕的事情會發生呢？

目録

1 賽姬公主

賽姬是國王最美麗的么女

p. 8

從前，有個國王，
他有三位漂亮的女兒。
英俊的男士紛紛從遠方慕名而來，
希望娶得美嬌娘。
賽姬是么女，最爲貌美。
人們不辭千里而來，只爲一睹風采。

- **once** [wʌns] 曾經
- **travel** [`trævl]
  遊歷；旅行
- **far away** [fɑːr ə`weɪ]
  遠遠地；遠處地
- **prettiest** [`prɪtɪst]
  最美麗的（pretty美麗；
  prettier較美麗的）

p. 9

美神阿芙柔黛蒂因此忌妒在心，
男人忽略淡忘她，
一心只想來看賽姬。
沒多久，
她的神廟就變得門可羅雀了，
因此，她決定要懲罰賽姬。

- **jealous** [dʒeləs] 妒忌的
- **ignore** [ɪg`nɔːr]
  忽視；不理會
- **empty** [empti]
  空的；無人的
- **decided to** [dɪ`saɪdɪd tuː]
  決定去……
- **punish** [pʌnɪʃ] 懲罰

p. 10

阿芙柔黛蒂對兒子愛羅斯說道：
「你必須去懲罰賽姬，
因為她，人們都遺忘我了，
我才是美麗女神！
讓賽姬愛上一個醜陋、噁心的怪物吧！
讓每個人都來嘲笑她！」

- **forget** [fərget] 忘記
- **beauty** [ˋbjuːti] 美麗
- **fall in love with**
  [fɔːl ɪn lʌv wɪθ]
  愛上……
- **ugly** [ʌgli] 醜陋的
- **disgusting** [dɪsˋgʌstɪŋ]
  噁心的；討厭的
- **creature** [ˋkriːtʃə(r)]
  生物；怪物
- **laugh at** [læf æt]
  嘲笑……

---

p. 11

愛羅斯來到阿芙柔黛蒂的花園中，
他看到那裡有兩座噴泉，
一座噴出甘甜的泉水，
另一座卻噴出苦澀的泉水。
甘甜之泉能讓女子變得更加美麗，
苦澀之泉則會招致危險。
女子如果碰觸了苦澀之泉，
將沒有男人會愛上她。
愛羅斯拿出兩個瓶子，
分別裝上甘甜之水和苦澀之水。

- **fountain** [faʊntn] 噴泉
- **sweet** [swiːt] 甜；甘美
- **the other** [ði ˋʌðə(r)]
  另一個
- **bitter** [bɪtə(r)] 苦的；
- **dangerous** [deɪndʒərəs]
  危險的
- **touch** [tʌtʃ] 觸碰
- **no man** [noʊ mæn]
  沒有人
- **ever** [evə(r)]
- **bottle** [ˋbɑːtl] 瓶子
- **put . . . in** [pʊt ɪn]
  放進；裝進

p. 12

愛羅斯來到賽姬的閨房，
賽姬此時正在熟睡。
愛羅斯一見到賽姬，
便對這美麗的女子一見傾心，
愛羅斯不忍讓她遭遇麻煩，
但他必須服從阿芙柔黛蒂，
因此他將苦澀之水，沾在賽姬唇上，
然後用弓箭推了推賽姬的手臂。

- **as soon as** [əz suːn əz]
  一……就……
- **was filled with**
  [wəz fild wɪθ]
  充滿；填滿
- **felt sorry** [felt sɑːri]
  覺得過意不去的
- **trouble** [ˈtrʌbl]
  麻煩事；困難
- **obey** [əˈbeɪ] 服從
- **drop** [drɑːp]
  一滴；少許
- **push** [pʊʃ] 推

p. 13

賽姬隨之醒來，
但她看不見隱形的愛羅斯。
愛羅斯見到賽姬美麗的雙眼，
更覺驚為天人。

- **woke up** [wok ʌp]
  醒來
- **invisible** [ɪnˈvɪzəbl]
  隱形的
- **was surprised**
  [wəz sərˈpraɪzd]
  感到驚訝的
- **saw** [sɔː]
  看見（see的過去式）

p. 14

當賽姬起身而坐時，
愛羅斯趕緊從床邊跳開，
結果不小心摔了跤，
被自己的弓箭給傷到了。
他一躍而起，
將甘甜之水倒在賽姬的秀髮上。
這甘甜之水與苦澀之水混合在一起，
讓賽姬的處境更加悽慘：
她變得更加貌美，
卻沒有男人會愛上她。

----

p. 15

接下來幾個月裡，
這位小公主又傷心又寂寞。
她等待著能有英俊瀟灑的王子前來求婚，
卻始終盼望不成。

她的兩個姐姐嫁給一對兄弟王子，
她們住進了王子的城堡中，
留下了賽姬獨自一人，
讓她更加倍覺孤單寂寞了。

- **sat up** [sæt ʌp] 坐起身來
- **jump away**
  [dʒʌmp əˋweɪ] 跳開
- **fell down** [fel daʊn]
  跌倒；跌落
- **himself** [hɪmˋself] 他自己
- **own** [oʊn] 自己的
- **jump up** [dʒmp ʌp] 跳起
- **pour . . . over**
  [pɔː(r) ˋoʊvə(r)]
  倒在……之上
- **mixture** [ˋmɪkstʃə(r)]
  混合
- **terrible** [ˋterəbl] 糟透了的

- **follow** [ˋfɑːloʊ]
  接續在……之後
- **lonely** [loʊnli] 寂寞
- **ask** [æsk] 請求
- **lonelier** [ˋloʊnli(r)]
  越來越寂寞
  （loneliest 最寂寞的）

p. 16

既是凡人女子，
就不該美若天仙，
賽姬的父母認為，
眾神正是因此才對她發怒的。
她的父母來到阿波羅神殿問神，
神諭說：
「令媛不會嫁給任何男人，
她會跑去山頂上，成為怪物的妻子。」

- **believe** [bɪˋliːv] 相信
- **as beautiful as**
  [əz ˋbjuːtɪfl əz]
  如……一樣美麗
- **advice** [ədˋvaɪs]
  忠告；建議；勸告
- **oracle** [ˋɔːrəkl]
  神諭
- **instead** [ɪnˋsted]
  取而代之
- **the top of** [ðə tɑːp əv]
  在……的頂部

p. 17

賽姬的父母一聽，便哭了起來，
他們承諾賽姬說，
他們才不會讓她去給怪物做妻子的。
但賽姬知道自己宿命難逃，
便準備到鄰近的山上去。
她聽說，那座山上住了一頭怪物。

- **promise** [ˋprɑːmɪs] 承諾
- **allow** [əˋlaʊ] 允許
- **escape** [ɪˋskep]
  逃脫；逃離
- **fate** [feɪt] 命運；宿命
- **prepare to** [prɪˋpe(r) tə]
  準備去……
- **nearby** [ˌnɪrˋbaɪ] 附近的
- **peak** [piːk]
  高峰的；頂點的

2 愛羅斯與賽姬之戀

在那個幸福的夜晚，他們在黑漆漆的房間裡成了親。

p. 18

賽姬走上山，
覺得自己是世上最孤單的女孩。
突然，
西風之神齊菲兒將她輕輕吹到空中，
帶她來到附近的草地上，
周圍群山圍繞。

- **climb** [klaɪm] 爬；攀登
- **felt like** [felt laɪk]
  感覺像……
- **was blown** [wəz blon]
  被風吹送
- **Zephyr** [ˋzefə(f)]
  西風之神齊菲兒
- **gently** [ˋdʒentli] 溫柔地
- **carry** [ˋkæri] 帶領
- **meadow** [ˋmedoʊ] 草地
- **surrounded by**
  [səˋraʊndɪd baɪ]
  被……圍繞

p. 19

這位年輕公主眨了眨眼，環顧四周。
她看到的不是可怕怪物住的洞穴，
而是在她的右手邊，
有一座被綠樹包圍著的泉水，
而在她的左手邊，
有一座蓋在山腰上的豪華皇宮。

- **blink** [blɪŋk] 眨
- **cave** [keɪv] 洞穴
- **fountain** [ˋfaʊntn] 噴泉
- **huge** [hjuːdʒ] 巨大的
- **hillside** [ˋhɪlsaɪd]
  山腰；山坡

p. 20

賽姬走進皇宮，
皇宮裡的家俱、雕像和繪畫飾品，
無不美輪美奐。

- **inside** [ˌɪnˋsaɪd]
  在內部的；室內的
- **furniture** [ˋfɜːrnɪtʃə(r)]
  傢具
- **sculpture** [ˋskʌlptʃə(r)]
  雕刻
- **painting** [ˋpeɪntɪŋ] 畫作
- **beautifully** [ˋbjuːtɪfli]
  美麗地
- **was made** [wəz meɪd]
  被製成……

---

p. 21

這是她聽到城堡中的某處傳來了聲音，
這聲音正對著她說話，
但她沒看到半個人影。
聲音說道：
「凡您所見，皆歸您所有。
我們是您的僕役，請儘管吩咐。
您是否要先在房中小憩片刻？
等您休息過後，梳洗完畢，
再來餐廳用膳。」

- **somewhere** [ˋsʌmwer]
  某個地方
- **yours** [jərz] 你的
- **servant** [ˋsɜːrvənt] 僕人
- **anything** [ˋeniθɪŋ]
  任何事情
- **lie down** [laɪ daʊn] 躺下
- **rest** [rest] 休息
- **ready** [ˋredi] 準備就緒的
- **take a bath** [teɪk ə bæθ]
  沐浴
- **dining room** [daɪnɪŋ rʊm]
  飯廳

p. 22

賽姬遵照著聲音的指示。
等她來到餐廳時，
她看到椅子在空中飛過，
然後停在餐桌前要給她坐。
那些看不見的手，
為她端來美味的食物和香甜的美酒。
一個看不見的樂隊，
開始演奏起和諧的樂音。
〔圖〕隱形僕役侍奉賽姬

- **suggested** [sə`dʒestɪd] 建議（suggest的過去式）
- **was placed** [wɑːz pleɪst] 被放置於……
- **in front of** [ɪn frʌnt əv] 在……之前
- **brought** [brɔt] 帶領（bring的過去式）
- **delicious** [dɪ`lɪʃəs] 美味的
- **delightful** [dɪ`laɪtfl] 愉快的
- **wine** [waɪn] 酒
- **orchestra** [`ɔːrkɪstrə] 樂器
- **soothing** [suːðɪŋ] 和緩的；有安慰作用的

p. 23

用過餐後，賽姬回到房中，
在黑暗中坐著。
不久，她聽到一個溫柔的聲音，
這個很輕柔，充滿了愛意，
和其他的聲音很不一樣。
那個聲音自稱他是城堡的主人。

- **returned to** [rɪ`tɜːrnd tu] 返回
- **dark** [dɑːrk] 黑暗
- **different from** [`dɪfrənt frʌm] 有別於……
- **loving** [`lʌvɪŋ] 有愛情的；深情的
- **owner** [`ounə(r)] 所有者

p. 24

「請別害怕。

我不是怪物，我是神。

我只有在黑暗的夜裡才能來看妳，

因為，凡人是不能直視神的。

我帶妳來這裡，是因為我愛妳。

當我第一眼看到妳，我便愛上妳了。

我希望能娶妳為妻，

但令人難過的是，

妳卻不能看到我的樣子。

不過，

我每天晚上都會在這個房間裡陪妳。」

這個講話者就是愛神愛羅斯，

但他沒讓賽姬知道。

賽姬感到一陣平靜，

旋即進入夢鄉。

- **be afraid of**
  [bi ə`freɪd əv]
  害怕……
- **person** [`pɜːrsn] 人
- **sadly** [`sædlɪ]
  悲哀地；不幸地
- **however** [hau`evə(r)]
  然而
- **with** [wɪθ]
  和……在一起
- **actually** [`æktʃuəlɪ]
  實際上；也就是
- **peace** [piːs] 安寧；平和
- **quickly** [`kwɪklɪ] 快速地
- **fell into a deep sleep**
  [fel `ɪntə ə diːp sliːp]
  進入深沉的睡眠

p. 25

隔天早晨，
賽姬醒來發現自己仍是孤單一人。
當她走出臥房，又傳來聲音，
要她把這裡當作自己的家，
一整天，
她就由這群隱形的僕役侍候著。

- **woke up** [wok ʌp]
  起來（wake up的過去式）
- **next** [nekst] 下一個
- **realize** [ˋrɪəlaɪz]
  了解；明白
- **alone** [əˋloun] 獨自
- **relax** [rɪlæks] 放鬆
- **serve** [sɜːrv] 侍候

p. 26

日復一日，僕役服侍著賽姬。
每到了晚上，
愛羅斯就會在房中對她說說話。
愛羅斯對她總是輕聲柔語的，
不久之後，賽姬也愛上了愛羅斯。

- **day after day**
  [deɪ ˋæftə(r) deɪ]
  日復一日
- **every** [ˋevri] 每一……
- **spoke** [spouk] 說；講
  （speak的過去式）
- **word** [wɜːrd] 話語
- **grew to** [gru tu]
  逐漸變得……；
  成為……
  （grow to的過去式）

13

p. 27

〔圖〕愛羅斯與賽姬
賽姬雖然不能見到愛羅斯的模樣，
但她仍愛著他。
能聽著他的聲音，她已經心滿意足，
他們在一起時，總是快樂又愜意。

就在這樣一個愉快的夜晚，
他們黑漆漆的房間裡成親了。

- **even though** [ˋiːvn ðoʊ]
  僅管如此
- **enough** [ɪˋnʌf] 足夠
- **comfortable** [ˋkʌmfətbl]
  舒適
- **got married** [gɑt ˋmærɪd]
  結婚了
  （got為get的過去式）
- **their** [ðer] 他們的

----

p. 28

在這個皇宮裡，賽姬衣食不缺，
她要什麼就有什麼。
然而，她不久就開始感到無聊，
希望能回家探望父母和姐姐。

- **nothing** [ˋnʌθɪŋ]
  什麼都不……；毫不
- **given** [ˋgɪvn] 被給予
- **became** [bɪˋkem]
  變成；成為
- **bored** [bɔːrd] 無聊

p. 29

一天夜裡，
賽姬告訴丈夫愛羅斯，
「我愛你，
願意與你終身廝守在這美麗的宮廷裡，
可是在白天裡，我的日子了無生氣，
我想回去探望我的父母和姐姐，
我想告訴他們，我過得很快樂，
身體健康，
我也想告訴他們，
我有了一位好丈夫。
總之，我不希望他們為我擔心。」

- **husband** [`hʌzbənd]
  丈夫
- **stay with** [steɪ wɪð]
  與……待在一起
- **forever** [fər`evə(r)]
  永遠地；長久地
- **during** [`duərɪŋ]
  在整段時間中
- **healthy** [`helθi] 健康的
- **most of all** [moust ʌv ɔ:l]
  最重要的
- **worry about**
  [`wɜːri ə`baut]
  對……感到擔心

p. 30

愛羅斯能了解賽姬的心情，
同意讓她邀請兩位姐姐前來。
他命令『西風』，
去將她的兩位姐姐帶來。

- **understood** [ˌʌndə`stud]
  明瞭；曉得
  （understand的過去式）
- **agree to** [ə`gri: tu]
  同意於……
- **order . . . to** [`ɔ:rdə(r) tu]
  命令……去

p. 31

賽姬一見到姐姐們，
就抱住她們，哭了起來。
「請跟我進到我家，
這裡什麼都不缺。
今晚，我們要設宴來慶祝團圓。」
賽姬說道。
賽姬帶著姐姐們逛了華麗皇宮。
她們參觀了富麗堂皇的房間，
看到各種雕像和珠寶箱。

- **met** [mɛt]
  相會（meet的過去式）
- **hug** [hʌg] 擁抱
- **feast** [fi:st] 宴會
- **celebrate** [ˋsɛlɪbreɪt]
  慶祝
- **reunion** [ri:ˋju:niən]
  團圓；聚會
- **show . . . around**
  [ʃoʊ əˋraʊnd]
  帶……參觀
- **finely** [ˋfaɪnli] 精巧地
- **decorated** [ˋdɛkəreɪtɪd]
  經過裝飾的
- **treasure** [ˋtrɛʒə(r)]
  金銀財寶
- **chest** [tʃɛst]
  一滿箱（的量）

p. 32

姐姐們看了，不由地嫉妒了起來，
吃晚餐時，
她們向賽姬打聽了她的丈夫。
她們很納悶，
為什麼主人沒有出現歡迎賓客呢？

- **strange** [streɪndʒ]
  奇怪的
- **introduce** [ˌɪntrəˋdu:s]
  介紹
- **yet** [jɛt]
  至今尚未；仍未

16

p. 33

「他是個英俊的年輕王子，
妳們可能看不到他了，
他白天通常都外出打獵，
晚上時才會回到家中。」
賽姬說道。
但兩位姐姐不肯罷休地說道：
「我們必須見到他本人，
向他問好，
才能對父母有所交代。」
賽姬不願對父母和姐姐撒謊，
便說道：「老實說，
我也沒見過他，
他只有在深夜一片漆黑中，
才會走進房間，
然後在天未亮之前就離開。
不管我怎麼請求，
他就是不肯讓我看到他的樣子。」

* **may** [meɪ]
  可能；也說不定
* **stay** [steɪ] 停留的時間
* **usually** [ju:dʒuəli] 通常
* **all day long** [ɔːl deɪ lɔːŋ]
  一整天
* **satisfied** [ˋsætɪsfaɪd]
  滿意的
* **must** [məst] 必需
* **lie** [laɪ] 說謊
* **frankly speaking**
  [ˋfræŋkli] 坦白地說
* **only** [ˋounli] 僅；只
* **enter** [ˋentə(r)] 進入
* **leave** [liːv] 離去；離開
* **dawn** [dɔːn] 黎明；破曉
* **no matter how**
  [nou ˋmætə(r) hau]
  不論如何
* **allow** [əˋlau] 允許；准許

p. 34

「難道這是眞的？」其中一位姐姐說道：
「他一定是隻可怕的怪物。
他爲什麼不讓妳看到他的長相呢？
有人跟我說，這附近住了一隻怪獸，
搞不好妳丈夫就是那隻怪獸！
我們要查出眞相！」

- **must** [məst] 必需
- **said** [sed]
  ……說（say的過去式）
- **maybe** [ˈmeɪbi]
  也許；大概
- **find out** [faɪnd aʊt]
  找出（答案）；揭露出
  （眞面目）

p. 35

「妳把燈和利刃藏在妳的房間裡，
待妳丈夫熟睡之後，
妳就用燈照他的臉。
若他果眞是一隻可怕怪物，
妳一定要殺了它。
到時候，妳就可以恢復自由，
回到我們身邊了。」
賽姬相信，她的丈夫不會是怪物的。
不過她也覺得奇怪，
爲什麼丈夫就是不讓她看到他的樣子。
於是，她決定在房間裡藏上一盞燈。

- **lantern** [ˈlæntərn] 提燈
- **sharp** [ʃɑːrp] 尖銳的
- **knife** [naɪf] 匕首；刀子
- **fall asleep** [fɔːll əsliːp]
  進入夢鄉
- **shine** [ʃaɪn]
  將（燈的）光射向
- **light** [laɪt] 光線
- **upon** [əpɑːn]
  在……之上
- **horrible** [hɔːrəbl]
  令人恐懼的
- **free** [friː] 自由
- **return** [rɪtɜːrn] 重返

p. 36

當晚，當丈夫熟睡之後，
她便將燈點亮，
把燈舉起來照丈夫。
她並沒有看到可怕的怪物，
她看到的，
是一位年輕、英俊的神，
他有著一頭金髮，膚色白晳，
還有一對雪白的翅膀。

賽姬這才知道，
她的丈夫就是愛羅斯，
愛羅斯俊美的臉龐令她著迷，
讓她心跳開始加速。
她彎下身子，
想看得更仔細一些。
結果，油燈裡的熱油
不小心滴到了愛羅斯的胸膛上。

----

p. 37

〔圖〕賽姬手持著燈

- **was asleep** [wɑːz əsliːp]
  在睡夢中
- **lit** [lɪt] 點燃；點火
  （light的過去式）
- **held** [hɛld]
  拿（hold的過去式）
- **golden** [ɡoʊldən] 金色的
- **wing** [wɪŋ] 翅膀；翼
- **realize** [rɪəlaɪz]
  了解；體會
- **charmed** [ˋtʃɑrmd]
  著迷的
- **began** [bɪˋɡæn] 開始
  （begin的過去式）
- **beat** [bit]
  （連續的）敲打
- **rapidly** [ræpɪdlɪ] 急促地
- **bend down** [bɛnd daʊn]
  彎下腰
- **closer** [kloʊsə] 較接近的
  （close靠近的；closest最
  靠近的）
- **look** [lʊk] 看；注視
- **a drop of** [ə drɑːp əv]
  一滴……
- **fell onto** [fɛl ɑːntə]
  落在……之上
  （fall的過去式）
- **chest** [tʃɛst] 胸部

19

3　賽姬的懲罰

「在我原諒妳之前，妳將辛苦贖罪。」

p. 38

愛羅斯醒來，不發一語，
便起身從窗口飛出。
「啊，傻賽姬！
妳為什麼要看我的臉呢？
彷彿妳信任愚蠢的姐姐，
更甚於信任自己的丈夫。
走吧，去跟她們一起渡過餘生吧。
缺樂信任的婚姻，
是無法持久的。」他說。
愛羅斯說完便飛走了，
他留下賽姬一個人，
任她倒在地上哭泣著。

- **without** [wɪðˋaʊt]
  不曾；沒有
- **stood up** [stʊd ʌp]
  站起來
  （stand up的過去式）
- **flew out of** [flu aʊt əv]
  飛出去……
  （flew是fly的過去式）
- **foolish** [ˋfulɪʃ] 傻的
- **It seems that . . .**
  [ˋɪt sims ðæt]
  似乎是……
- **trust** [trʌst] 相信；信任
- **silly** [sɪli] 愚蠢的
- **more than** [mor ðən]
  比……多
- **spend** [spɛnd]
  花費（時間）；度過
- **rest** [rɛst]
  剩餘的；往後的
- **last** [læst] 繼續；持續
- **lying** [ˋlaɪɪŋ] 躺著的
- **ground** [graʊnd]
  地上的；地面的

p. 39

頃刻間，賽姬發現自己身處空曠的大地
上。姐姐們的城堡就在一旁。
賽姬走進入城堡，
告訴她們事情發過的經過。
姐姐們虛情假意地為賽姬感到難過，
但實際上她們是幸災樂禍的。
她們心想，
這下子愛羅斯就會從她們兩個姐姐當中
選一個人來與他成親了。

- **instantly** [ˋɪnstəntlɪ]
  立即地；馬上地
- **open** [oʊpən] 空曠的
- **field** [fild] 域；場
- **whole** [hol]
  整個的；全部的
- **pretend to** [prɪˋtɛnt tə]
  假裝要……裝作要……
- **perhaps** [pəˋhæps]
  或許；大概
- **choose** [tʃouz] 選擇

p. 40

隔天早晨，兩位姐姐醒來，
暗中打包好行李。
她們兩人都打算要去愛羅斯的城堡。
大姐先動身出發了。
她來到山頂，呼喚「西風」，
然後躍身跳下，以為西風會將她接住，
帶她去愛羅斯那裡。
然而，西風並沒有前來，
大姐於是重重摔下而死了。

二姐稍後來到，她和大姐做了
同樣的事情，也因此摔死了。

- **pack** [pæk] 打包
- **quietly** [ˋkwaɪətlɪ]
  安靜地
- **both** [bouθ]
  兩者；雙方（都）
- **plan to** [plæn tu]
  計畫要……
- **left** [lɛft] 離開
  （leave的過去式）
- **reach** [ritʃ] 達到
- **call for** [kɔl fə(r)]
  大聲呼叫
- **jump off** [dʒʌmp ɔːf]
  跳下
- **hill** [hɪl] 山丘

21

p. 41

過了一些日子，賽姬收起難過心情，
決定去找丈夫，請求他原諒。
她對自己發誓說：
沒有找到愛羅斯，就誓不放棄。

這天早晨，
賽姬整理好包袱後，
便出發找尋丈夫。
幾週之後，她來到一座高山，
山頂上有一間神廟。
賽姬心想，丈夫也許就住在神廟裡，
於是她就走進了神廟。

- recovered from [rɪˋkʌvəd ˋfrɑːm] 從……恢復正常
- sadness [ˋsædnɪs] 悲傷
- forgiveness [fəˋgɪvənəs] 原諒；寬恕
- promise oneself [ˋprɑmɪs wʌnˋsɛlf] 答應自己
- holy [ˋhoʊli] 聖潔的；神聖的

p. 42

進入神廟後，
賽姬看到地上堆滿玉米和麥穗，
其中還放有一些農具。
賽姬是個信仰虔誠的人，
她不忍看到這麼一個莊嚴華麗的神廟，
卻一團髒亂，
便開始清理起玉米和麥穗，
撿起散落一地的農具。

- corn [kɔːrn] 穀物；小麥
- barley [ˋbɑːrlɪ] 大麥
- all over [ˋɔl ovər] 到處；遍布
- tool [tul] 工具；器具
- lying in a mess [ˋlaɪɪŋ ɪn ə mes] 躺在混亂之中
- religious [rɪˋlɪdʒəs] 宗教上的
- messy [ˋmesi] 凌亂的
- sweep(up) [swip ˋʌp] 打掃；掃除
- pick up [pɪk ˋʌp] 收拾；整理

p. 43

原來這是女神狄蜜特的神殿。

此時，女神狄蜜特正好經過。

女神看著用心清理神殿的賽姬，

不禁升起愛憐之心。

「賽姬，

我知道妳最近所遭遇的事情，

我也希望能夠幫助妳，只是，

我無法讓阿芙柔黛蒂平息對妳的怒火。

我能做的，

就是告訴妳要怎麼做：

妳去阿芙柔黛蒂的神廟，

告訴她妳很尊敬她，

祈求她原諒妳。或許，

這樣她就會讓妳再見到她的兒子愛羅斯

了。」

- **belong(to)** [bɪlɔːŋ]
  屬於……所有
- **Demeter** [dɪˋmitə]
  狄蜜特（希神）
- **at that moment**
  [æt ðæt ˋmomənt]
  此刻；當時
- **pass(by)** [pæs ˋbaɪ]
  從……旁經過
- **pity** [ˋpɪti] 憐憫；同情
- **clean** [klin] 使整潔
- **suffer** [ˋsʌfə(r)] 受苦痛
- **lately** [ˋletlɪ] 近來
- **the best thing**
  [ðə bɛst θɪŋ] 最好的
- **advice** [ədˋvaɪs]
  建議；忠告
- **respect** [rɪˋspekt]
  尊敬；敬重

p. 44

賽姬於是來到阿芙柔黛蒂的神殿。
女神一副對她很生氣的樣子。
「妳是來敬拜我的嗎？」
阿芙柔黛蒂問道：
「還是，妳想見的是妳的丈夫，
而不是我？」
我可憐的兒子，爲了妳而心碎，
所以我要懲罰妳。
在我原諒妳之前，妳將辛苦贖罪。
之後，
也許妳就可以再見到妳的丈夫了。

- **seem** [si:m] 似乎；好像
- **worship** [ˋwɜːʃəp] 參拜；敬奉
- **instead of** [ɪnˋstd əv] 取而代之
- **broken heart** [ˋbrokən hɑrt] 破碎的心
- **before** [brˋfo(r)] 在……之前

p. 45

阿芙柔黛蒂指著一大堆的豆子、大麥、
小麥和穀粒。
「妳要將穀粒分類，
把不同的穀粒，放在不同的袋子裡，
天黑之前要把它完成。」
說完，阿芙柔黛蒂便離開了。

賽姬跪倒在地上，哭了起來。
她知道自己是無法完成任務的。

- **heap of** [hip əv] 一堆；大量
- **bean** [bin] 豆子
- **wheat** [wit] 小麥
- **grain** [greɪn] 穀物
- **separate** [ˋsæpərət] 分開
- **nightfall** [ˋnaɪtˌfɔ:l] 黃昏；日暮

p. 46

有一隻小螞蟻，覺得賽姬很可憐，
便吆喝其他同伴，
幫助這位美麗的女子。
螞蟻們同意幫忙，
女王蟻便將工蟻分組，
每一組負責搜集一種穀類。
螞蟻們像軍隊一樣，
對著穀類出發前進，
將穀類搬至各自的袋子中。

---

p. 47

到黃昏時，工作就已經完成了。
阿芙柔黛蒂用過晚餐後，
便回來找她。
當她看到賽姬完成了工作，
她很失望。
「這顯然不是妳自己獨力完成的，
一定是我兒子來幫助妳的！」
阿芙柔黛蒂將一片腐壞的麵包，
朝著賽姬丟去，然後轉身離開。

- **felt sorry for**
  [fɛlt sɔːrɪ fɔːr] 可憐
- **organize** [ˈɔːrɡənˌaɪz]
  組織起來
- **was supposed to**
  [wəz səˈpoʊzd tu]
  應該；要
- **gather** [ˈɡæðər]
  聚合；聚集
- **kind of** [kaɪnd əv]
  一種；一類
- **march** [mɑːrtʃ]
  （齊步）前進
- **carry...into** [ˈkærɪ ɪntuː]
  搬運……進入
- **proper** [ˈprɑːpə(r)]
  適當的；妥當的

- **dusk** [dʌsk] 黃昏；傍晚
- **disappointed**
  [ˌdɪsəˈpɔɪntɪd]
  失望的；沮喪的
- **clearly** [ˈklɪrli]
  無疑的；明顯的
- **by yourself** [baɪ jərˈself]
  靠你自己之力
- **somehow** [ˈsʌmhaʊ]
  以某種方法；設法
- **threw** [θru]
  扔；擲（throw的過去式）
- **a piece of** [ə piːs əv]
  一片……（與不可數名詞連用作量詞）
- **rotten** [rɑːtn]
  腐爛的；發臭的

25

p. 48

隔天早晨，

阿芙柔黛蒂帶著賽姬來到附近的河岸。

「在對面的河岸上，

妳會看到長著金色羊毛的羊隻。

妳就去取下每一隻羊身上的一些羊毛吧，

天黑之前把羊毛帶回來給我看。」

- **riverbank** [ˈrɪvərbæŋk]
  河堤；河岸
- **ram** [ræm] 公羊
- **fleece** [fliːs] 羊毛
- **wool** [wʊl] 羊毛；毛線
- **make sure** [meɪk ʃʊr]
  確信；有把握
- **bring...back** [brɪŋ bæk]
  帶……回來

---

p. 49

賽姬來回徘徊，想找出渡河的辦法，

這河水又急又深。

突然，河神現身對她說道：

「親愛的賽姬，

不要在這個時候過河。

在這個時候過河，羊群會攻擊妳的。

牠們會用尖牙利角攻擊人類。

等到中午時，河水平靜了，

妳那時候再過河就很容易了。

河岸對面的羊群，也會開始入睡。

那樣妳就可以在矮樹叢和樹幹上，

會找到足夠的金羊毛了。」

- **back and forth**
  [bæk ənd fɔːrθ] 來回徘徊
- **cross** [krɔːs] 橫越；跨過
- **spoke** [spoʊk] 說話
  （speak的過去式）
- **dear** [dɪr] 親愛的；可愛的
- **hurt** [hɜːt] 傷害
- **horn** [hɔːrn] （羊）角
- **calm** [kɑːm] 平靜
- **able to** [ˈeɪbl tə] 能夠……
- **easily** [ˈiːzəli] 輕易地
- **fast** [fæst] 快速的
- **bush** [bʊʃ] 灌木矮樹
- **trunk** [trʌŋk] 軀幹；樹幹
- **plenty of** [ˈplen ti əv]
  充裕的……；足夠的

p. 50

賽姬便跟著指示所說的來做。

很快地，

她就收集到了大量的金羊毛。

她將羊毛帶回去給阿芙柔黛蒂，

女神看到看到賽姬完成了使命，

一陣不悅。

「我想，這次一定又有人從中幫忙。」

- **follow** [ˋfɑ:loʊ]
  聽從；跟隨
- **a lot of** [ə lɑ:t əv]
  許多的；大量的
- **pleased** [pli:zd]
  令人高興；討人喜歡
- **once again** [wʌnts əgen]
  再一次
- **guess** [ges] 推測；猜測
- **somebody** [sʌmbədi]
  某人；有人

---

p. 51

「我要妳再為我做一件事情，

妳下到冥界，去找冥后泊瑟芬，

告訴她，

是我要妳去取回一些她的美貌的。

我在照顧生病的愛羅斯時，

喪失了一些美貌。

快去快回，

我要在今晚的眾神宴會開始之前，

用她的美貌來裝扮自己一下。」

- **thing** [θɪŋ] 事情
- **underworld**
  [ʌndərwɜ:ld] 地獄；冥界
- **collect** [kəˋlekt] 收集
- **beauty** [ˋ.] 美麗
- **lost** [lɔ:st] 失去；損失
  （lost的過去式）
- **while** [waɪl]
  當……；在……的時候
- **nurse** [nɜ:rs]
  看護（病人）；調養
  （疾病）
- **sick** [sɪk] 生病的；身體
  不舒服的
- **hurry** [ˋhɜ:ri] （使）趕緊
- **paint** [peɪnt]
  裝飾；給……加色

p. 52

賽姬必須立即下到冥界。
要到冥界，她只知道一條捷徑：
殺了她自己。
因此，她爬上一座高塔，
正當她準備往下跳之時，
傳來了一個聲音。
聲音說道：
「妳何必用這種危險的方式，
下到冥界去呢？」

- **reach** [ri:tʃ] 到達
- **immediately** [ɪmi:diətli] 即刻；馬上
- **knew** [nui] 知道（know的過去式）
- **get** [get] 使到達（目的地）
- **quickly** [kwɪkli] 快速地
- **climb** [klaɪm] 爬上
- **just** [dʒʌst] 正好；恰恰
- **in such a way** [ɪn sʌtʃ ə weɪ] 用如此……的方式

p. 53

「我知道有一個比較簡單的方法，
用走的就可以下到冥界了。」
這聲音還告訴她如何說服冥界擺渡者，
讓她渡過守誓河。
聲音告訴賽姬，在洞穴中的一條通道，
這條通道可以躲過守衛冥界入口的三頭犬。
「但是妳要小心！」聲音說：
「泊瑟芬會給妳一個盒子，
盒子裡面會裝著她的美麗，
妳絕對不可以偷看。
不管妳有多好奇，
都不可以偷看盒內之物。」

- **on foot** [ɑːn fʊt] 以步行
- **convince** [kənˋvɪns] 說服
- **ferryman** [ˋferimən] 渡船工人
- **Styx** [stɪks] 守誓河
- **path** [pæθ] 通道；小徑
- **cave** [keɪv] 山洞；洞穴
- **past** [pæst] 越過
- **three headed** [θriː hedɪd] 三頭的
- **guard** [gɑːrd] 守衛
- **entrance** [ˋenˋtrænts] 入口
- **containing** [kənˋteɪnɪŋ] 容納；裝；盛
- **no matter how** [noʊ ˋmæt.ɚ haʊ] 不論如何
- **curious** [kjʊiəs] 好奇的

28

p. 54

賽姬遵照聲音指示，
來到冥界。
泊瑟芬親切地問候她，
女神很樂意幫忙。
她將一個盒子遞給賽姬。
賽姬恭敬地謝過泊瑟芬。

接著，她沿著原路回去。
安全地回到人間。

- **did** [dɪd]
  做（do的過去式）
- **exactly** [ɪgˋzæktli]
  正確地；嚴密地
- **as** [əz] 同……一樣
- **greet** [griːt] 迎接；問候
- **warmly** [ˋwɔːrmlɪ]
  熱情地
- **politely** [pəlaɪtli]
  有禮貌地；有教養地
- **turn** [tɜːrn]
  拐入；轉向
- **safely** [ˋseflɪ]
  平安地；安全地

----

p. 55

在回去的漫長路途中，
她開始對盒子感到好奇。
賽姬看著盒子許久，最後，她想，
「盒子是我拿到手的，
所以我也可以使用其中的美麗。
如果我讓自己變得更美，
那樣愛羅斯就會再次愛上我的。」
賽姬於是打開盒子，
可是她卻沒有看到美麗，
只看到有一股紫色氣體流逸出來，
縈繞在她的腦際，
讓她沈沈睡去。

- **stare(at)** [ster æt]
  盯；凝視
- **for a long time** [fə(r) ə
  lɔːŋ taɪm] 一段長時間
- **use** [juːz] 使用
- **purple** [pɜːrpl] 紫色的
- **gas** [gæs] 氣（體）
- **came out** [keɪm aʊt]
  跑出來（came是come的
  過去式）
- **surround** [səraʊnd]
  圍繞；圍住
- **fall asleep** [fɑːl əsliːp]
  進入睡眠

愛羅斯的寬恕

「我要找回我的妻子。」

p. 56

這期間，愛羅斯也振作了起來，
決心要原諒賽姬。
「我要找回我的妻子。」他說。
這時他發現賽姬躺在路上熟睡著，
他將紫色氣體，從賽姬頭上吹開，
讓氣體回到盒子裡，然後喚醒賽姬。
「妳太過於好奇了，
把盒子拿回去給我的母親吧，
我會請求宙斯讓我們復合的。

- **meanwhile** [mi:n.waɪl]
  在此同時
- **recover from**
  [rɪkʌvər frəm]
  從……恢復
- **broken heart**
  [brou.kən hɑ:rt]
  破碎的心
- **decide** [dɪ`saɪd] 決定
- **in the middle of**
  [ɪn ðə `mɪdl əv]
  在……的中間
- **blew** [blu:]
  吹走（blow的過去式）
- **woke up** [wouk ʌp] 醒來
  （wake up的過去式）
- **too** [tu:] 太……
- **shall** [ʃæl] 應；必須

p. 57

愛羅斯飛去找宙斯。

「啊！宙斯，眾神之王！

我請求你讓賽姬再度成為我的妻子！

我知道，凡人是不能和神結婚的，

但是這位公主，

有著女神的風采和美貌，

她會是我的好妻子的。

我知道，她有許多凡人的缺點。」

他繼續說道：

「她最大的缺點，就是她的好奇心，

好奇心驅使她去看我的臉。

但是，別忘了，

正是你在創造女人時，

給了她們好奇心的。」

- **flew** [flu:]
  飛（fly的過去式）
- **manners** [mænərz] 舉止
- **grace** [greɪs] 優雅
- **human** [hju:mən] 凡人
- **weakness** [wi:knəs] 缺點
- **continue** [kən`tɪn.ju:]
  繼續
- **greatest** [greɪtɪst] 最大的
- **curiosity** [kjuəri`ɑ:sə.ti]
  好奇心
- **remember** [rɪ`meɪmbər]
  記住

p. 58

愛羅斯和宙斯談了幾個小時，
最後，宙斯答應了愛羅斯。
他讓賽姬參加眾神之宴，
當賽姬抵達時，
宙斯給她一杯有法力的酒。
「賽姬，喝下它，妳就會成為神了。」
宙斯說道：
「妳和愛羅斯就可以再結為連理，
白頭偕老，直到永遠。」
賽姬於是接過酒杯，將酒喝下。

- **agree with** [əgri: wɪð]
  同意；認同
- **arrive** [əraɪv] 抵達
- **magical** [ˋmædʒɪkəl]
  有法力的；神奇的
- **wine** [waɪn] 酒
- **a cup of wine**
  [ə kʌp əv waɪn]
  一杯酒
- **drank** [dræŋk]
  喝；飲（drink的過去式）

---

p. 59

天使歡唱，
愛羅斯和賽姬終於復合。
時至今日，
他們仍然相守在一起。
除了他們的女兒，
他們大概是最幸福的神仙了。
他們的女兒，
名字就叫做「歡愉」。

- **sang** [sæŋ] 歌唱
  （sing的過去式）
- **even** [i:vn] 即使
- **perhaps** [pərhæps] 或許
- **happier** [hæpiər]
  更快樂的（happy快樂的）
- **daughter** [dɔ:tər] 女兒
- **pleasure** [pledʒər]
  愉快；高興

閱讀測驗

※ 閱讀下列問題並選出最適當的答案。 ➡ 60-63 頁

1. 為什麼阿芙柔黛蒂的神廟會乏人祭祀?

   (A) 因為阿芙柔黛蒂的忌妒心作祟。

   (B) 因為人們更喜歡去探望賽姬。

   (C) 因為阿芙柔黛蒂不漂亮了。

   答案 (B)

2. 當賽姬說她想見家人時,他的丈夫是如何反應的?

   (A) 他很傷心。

   (B) 他很生氣。

   (C) 他能理解。

   答案 (C)

3. 當賽姬舉起提燈,照向愛羅斯的臉龐時,她看見了什麼?

   (A) 一隻醜陋的怪獸。

   (B) 一位全身雪白的神。

   (C) 一位有著金髮的俊美神祇。

   答案 (C)

33

4. 賽姬的姐姐們聽到她與愛神分開時的真實感受是
什麼？

    (A) 她們覺得難過。

    (B) 她們覺得開心。

    (C) 她們很驚訝。

答案 (B)

5. 賽姬在狄密特的神廟中做了什麼事？

    (A) 清理地板。

    (B) 她在敬拜狄密特。

    (C) 她搞得一團亂。

答案 (A)

6. 阿芙柔黛蒂叫賽姬把一堆穀物做怎樣的處理？

    (A) 叫她想辦法讓螞蟻們把穀物分開。

    (B) 叫她把一大堆的穀物分成小堆小堆
        的穀物。

    (C) 叫她把不同的穀物分別放進各自的
        袋子裡。

答案 (C)

7. 誰帶賽姬到山坡上大宮殿裡去？
答案 _____.

答案 Zephyr

8. 賽姬的第二個懲罰是什麼？
答案 _____

_____

_____.

答案：Taking a little golden fleeces from every one of the rams and giving it to Aphrodite.

9. 泊瑟芬給賽姬的盒子裡裝有什麼東西？
答案 _____.

答案 purple gas

10. 愛神愛羅斯和賽姬的女兒叫什麼名字？
答案 _____.

答案 Pleasure

35

※ 閱讀下段文章，並討論之以下的問題。

……她們參觀了富麗堂皇的房間，看到各種雕像和珠寶箱，不由得心生妒忌。……她們佯裝為賽姬感到難過，但事實上她們感到很痛快。她們心想，這下子愛羅斯就會從她們兩個姐姐當中，選一個人來與他成親了。

11. 賽姬的兩個姐姐們之所以討厭賽姬，是因為心生妒忌。你是否也曾經忌妒過呢？如果是，試談論之。

參考答案

When I was 8 years old, I have hated my schoolmate.
Because she was prettier and wiser than me.

……在回去的漫長路途中，她開始對盒子感到好奇。賽姬看著盒子許久，最後，她想，「盒子是我拿到手的，所以我也可以使用其中的美麗。如果我讓自己變得更美，那樣愛羅斯就會再次愛上我的。」賽姬於是打開盒子……

12. 賽姬打開了不應該打開的盒子，因為她想要擁有更出色的美貌。假設你是賽姬，你會怎麼做？

參考答案

I wouldn't open the box.
I would stand next to Aphrodite when she opens the box.
Then the purple gas would paint beauty on my face, too.

黃道十二宮

黃道十二宮　➜ 64~68 頁

「黃道帶」（zodiac）這個字源自希臘文，意指「動物的環狀軌道」。黃道帶的起源爲何？在本篇裡，你將可以看到說明星座來源的希臘神話故事：

太陽（the Sun）、地球（the Earth）、牡羊座（the Ram）、金牛座（the Bull）、雙子座（the Twins）、巨蟹座（the Crab）、獅子座（the Lion）、處女座（the Virgin）、天秤座（the Balance）、天蠍座（the Scorpion）、射手座（the Archer）、摩羯座（the Goat）、寶瓶座（the Water Bearer）、雙魚座（the Fishes）。

1. Aries（the Ram）牡羊座
2. Libra（the Balance）天秤座
3. Taurus（the Bull）金牛座
4. Scorpio（the Scorpion）天蠍座
5. Gemini（the Twins）雙子座
6. Sagittarius（the Archer）射手座
7. Cancer（the Crab）巨蟹座
8. Capricorn（the Goat）摩羯座
9. Leo（The Lion）獅子座
10. Aquarius（the Water Bearer）寶瓶座
11. Virgo（the Virgin）處女座
12. Pisces（the Fishes）雙魚座

牡羊座（the Ram）　3.21-4.20

牡羊座源自於金羊毛的故事。白羊安全營救福里瑟斯，福里瑟斯把金羊獻祭給宙斯作為回報，宙斯便將金羊形象化為天上星座。

金牛座（the Bull）　4.21-5.20

金牛座源自於歐羅巴和公牛的故事。宙斯化身為公牛，以便吸引歐羅巴，公牛載著歐羅巴跨海來到克里特島。宙斯將公牛的形象化為星座，以為紀念。

雙子座（the Twins）　5.21-6.21

雙子座源自於卡斯特與波樂克斯的故事。他們兩人為孿生兄弟，彼此相親相愛。為了紀念其兄弟情誼，宙斯將他們的形象化為星座。

巨蟹座（the Crab）　6.22-7.22

巨蟹座源自於赫丘力的十二項苦差役。希拉派遣巨蟹前去殺害赫丘力，但是赫丘力在打敗九頭蛇之前，一腳將巨蟹踩碎。為了紀念巨蟹，希拉將其形象化為星座。

獅子座（The Lion）　7.23-8.22

獅子座亦源自於赫丘力十二項苦差中。赫丘力的第一項苦差，是要殺死奈米亞山谷之獅。他徒手殺了獅子，為了紀念這項偉大的事蹟，宙斯將奈米亞獅子的形象，置於星辰之中。

處女座（the Virgin）　8.23-9.22

處女座源自於潘朵拉的故事。處女指的是純潔與天真女神阿絲蒂雅。潘朵拉好奇將禁盒打開，讓許多邪惡事物來到人間，眾神紛紛返回天庭。為了紀念這種失落的純真，便把阿絲蒂雅的形象置於群星中。

天秤座（the Balance）　9.23-10.21

天秤是正義的秤子，由神聖正義女神蒂米絲隨身攜帶。天秤座落在處女座旁邊，因為阿絲蒂雅是蒂米絲之女。

天蠍座（the Scorpion）　10.22-11.21

天蠍座源自於歐里昂。歐里昂和阿蒂蜜絲是一對狩獵夥伴，阿蒂蜜絲的哥哥阿波羅對此忌妒不已。他請求蓋亞殺了歐里昂。因此，蓋亞創造天蠍殺了偉大的歐里昂。為了紀念此事，宙斯將歐里昂和天蠍化成星座。這兩個星座從來不會同時出現。

射手座（the Archer）　11.23-12.21

射手座代表卡隆。在希臘神話故事中，卡隆是許多英雄的朋友，例如亞吉力、赫丘力。赫丘力以毒箭誤傷了卡隆。卡隆是神，因此得以不死，但是卻必須忍受這無止盡的痛苦，所以卡隆央求宙斯殺了他。為了紀念卡隆，宙斯將他化為星座。

摩羯座 （the Goat） 12.22-1.19

魔羯代表哺育年幼宙斯的羊阿瑪爾夏。
據說宙斯為了感念此羊，將之化為星座。

寶瓶座 （the Water Bearer） 1.20-2.18

寶瓶座源自於鐸卡連的洪水。在這個故事中，宙
斯在人間降下豪雨，讓洪水沖走一切邪惡的生
物。只有鐸卡連和妻子皮雅是洪水的生還者。

雙魚座 （the Fishes） 2.19-3.20

雙魚座代表愛與美之女神阿芙柔黛蒂，
以及其子愛神愛羅斯。當時有個颱風，
兩人沿著優芙瑞特河步行。他們請求宙
斯援救，宙斯將兩人變成魚，讓他們安
然渡過風災。為了紀念此事，阿芙柔黛
蒂化身為星座中的大魚，愛羅斯則化為
小魚。

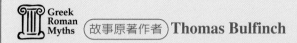
Greek Roman Myths 故事原著作者 **Thomas Bulfinch**

Without a knowledge of mythology much of the elegant literature of our own language cannot be understood and appreciated.

　　缺少了神話知識，就無法了解和透徹語言的文學之美。

—Thomas Bulfinch

　　Thomas Bulfinch（1796-1867），出生於美國麻薩諸塞州的Newton，隨後全家移居波士頓，父親爲知名的建築師Charles Bulfinch。他在求學時期，曾就讀過一些優異的名校，並於1814年畢業於哈佛。

　　畢業後，執過教鞭，爾後從商，但經濟狀況一直未能穩定。1837年，在銀行擔任一般職員，以此爲終身職業。後來開始進一步鑽研古典文學，成爲業餘作家，一生未婚。

　　1855年，時值59歲，出版了奠立其作家地位的名作*The Age of Fables*，書中蒐集希臘羅馬神話，廣受歡迎。此書後來與日後出版的 *The Age of Chivalry*（1858）和 *Legends of Charlemagne*（1863），合集更名爲 *Bulfinch's Mythology*。

　　本系列書系，即改編自 *The Age of Fable*。Bulfinch 著寫本書時，特地以成年大眾爲對象，以將古典文學引介給一般大眾。*The Age of Fable* 堪稱十九世紀的羅馬神話故事的重要代表著作，其中有很多故事來源，來自Bulfinch自己對奧維德（Ovid）的《變形記》（*Metamorphoses*）的翻譯。

■Bulfinch 的著作

1. Hebrew Lyrical History.
2. The Age of Fable: Or Stories of Gods and Heroes.
3. The Age of Chivalry.
4. The Boy Inventor: A Memoir of Matthew Edwards, Mathematical-Instrument Maker.
5. Legends of Charlemagne.
6. Poetry of the Age of Fable.
7. Shakespeare Adapted for Reading Classes.
8. Oregon and Eldorado.
9. Bulfinch's Mythology: Age of Fable, Age of Chivalry, Legends of Charlemagne.